Planet Kayterus

The Flying Orange

A Black Hole

The Space Giant's Beanstalk

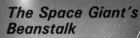

Oddball

Major Tom

Series 814

The Fun Guys Stories:

The Spring Time and the Moth Ball
The Hen Coat and the Ship Shape
The Rat Race and the Sky Lark
The Bottleneck and the Mole Hole
The Mush Rooms and the Fox Glove
The Mouse Trap and the Cricket Team

The Adventures of Major Tom:

The Planet of the Elves
The Missing Ambassador
The Space Pirates
The Fiery Space Dron
Space Invasion Skyhawk
The Deadly Plant Planet

First edition

© LADYBIRD BOOKS LTD MCMLXXXIV

Adventures of Major Tom

The Deadly Plant Planet

written and illustrated by PETER LONGDEN

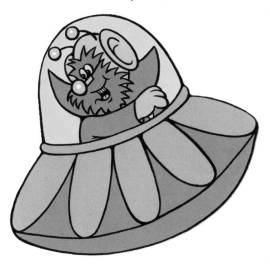

Ladybird Books Loughborough

The Flying Orange was once more high up in space and speeding towards the friendly planet of Rengo. The Space Federation had just received an SOS from the planet before communications were cut off. Major Tom and Oddball had been ordered to investigate the mysterious call for help.

Soon the orange was flying over the planet looking for the beautiful city from which the SOS call had been sent. But Tom could only see huge plants completely covering the surface of the planet and reaching high into the sky.

Then Oddball noticed a tower rising out of the jungle undergrowth. "There's the city," he said. "It's been completely overgrown with huge weeds!"

Oddball steered the orange to a safe landing place and the two crime-fighters stepped out.

"It's amazing! How have these plants grown so big and so quickly over a new city of this size?"

"I don't know," replied Tom, "but look at the wonderful flowers."

Tom climbed on a leaf and sniffed the sweet smelling flower.

Oddball suddenly noticed the head of the flower opening up.

"Be careful, sir!" he shouted.

9

SNAP! Too late! The flower head had closed and had begun to swallow Tom.

"Help!" gurgled Major Tom, as he struggled to escape. Oddball moved quickly and grabbed the Major's feet.

Then using all his strength, he pulled him to safety.

"That was a close shave, sir!" said Oddball.

"Yes!" said a dazed Tom. "I wonder what evil we are up against this time?"

Tom and Oddball moved on, fighting their way through the tangled jungle, being very careful to avoid the flowers!

At last they could see the palace of the emperor of the planet.

Forcing their way inside, they found a miserable emperor holding a meeting with his ministers.

"I'm Major Tom of the Space Federation. Can I help?"

"Oh, thank goodness you received our call for help," said the emperor. "We've heard tales of your brave deeds, Major Tom. You're our last hope."

The emperor told Tom and Oddball about how the fiendish space villain, Dr Plantro, had sprayed the city with an evil plant mixture. This had caused the giant weeds which had covered the city.

The emperor continued. "The people are trapped in their houses. The mono space rail is choked with weeds. Everywhere there is confusion – the planet is at a complete standstill.

"The doctor has given us one week to give him all the gold and silver in our city. In return for this he will give us a mixture to kill the weeds," said the emperor, finishing his story.

"Can't you make your own mixture to kill the weeds?" asked Tom.

"No," said one of the ministers. "Our scientists are working to find an answer, but so far...nothing!"

"Fear not!" said Tom. "We'll sort out this blackmailing doctor and come back and kill the weeds!"

The emperor and his ministers gave a mighty cheer as Tom and Oddball left for the Flying Orange.

17

18

As the orange blasted off from the Planet Rengo, Oddball plotted a course for the deadly floating island of Dr Plantro.

"Full warp speed, Oddball, we have no time to lose," said Tom bravely.

Eventually the Flying Orange reached its destination. Tom and Oddball gazed for the first time at the gloomy island that floated through space. This was the home of the dreaded Doctor.

''Prepare for touch down!'' shouted Oddball and the orange glided down to the creepy island in the sky.

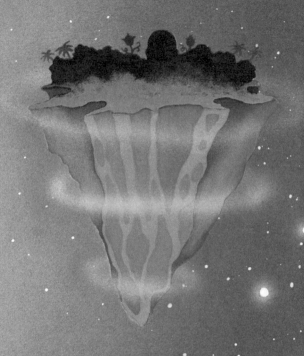

Tom and Oddball left their spaceship and were soon staring at the laboratory of their enemy. It was surrounded by a dense forest and inside the horrid hedge was a ring of the snapping flowers.

"Let's try and get through the forest," said Tom and he led the way slowly.

"I'm sure that tree just moved," remarked Oddball.

"It's your imagination," replied Tom, trying to look brave.

But Oddball was right. With an eerie screech, a tree jumped out at Tom and grabbed him with strong twiggy arms.

"Ugh, they're alive!" gasped Tom.

"Run, Oddball! Save yourself," shouted Major Tom, but the brave little robot was already thinking of a way to free Tom.

Tom struggled to break free as other trees started to close in on Oddball. The big clumsy tree holding Tom started to walk towards the laboratory. But the quick-thinking Oddball shot out one of his metal legs and tripped up the fearful creature.

As the tree crashed to the ground, it let go of Tom. Oddball and Major Tom breathed a sigh of relief as the big tree rolled over, shaking its fist and howling with rage.

"Are you all right, Major?" asked Oddball, as the two returned to the orange.

"Just a little scratched," came the reply. "That rough lump of wood's bark was worse than its bite!"

Back at the Flying Orange Tom and Oddball worked out a new plan to get at Dr Plantro. "Right," said Tom. "Into Segment One. If we can't get *through* Plantro's defences we'll just have to get *over* them!"

Segment One was soon speeding over
the spooky forest. "Let's head for that
window below the dome. Perhaps we
can sneak in," said Tom.

As Segment One hovered above the window, Tom dropped a rope ladder through a trap door in the mini ship and climbed down towards the open window.

Peering through, he could see the evil Doctor busily making more deadly mixtures.

The Doctor was laughing as he worked. "With the help of my jet spray plane, I'll be able to conquer the whole of the galaxy single-handed," he scoffed. "No one will stop me now. I'll be rich and powerful!"

"I'll stop you, Plantro," said Tom loudly, as he swung through the open window.

"Curses!" said Plantro. "Who are you?"

"I'm Major Tom of the Space Federation, and I arrest you for breaking galaxy rules!" came the reply.

"You'll never take me in," snarled Dr Plantro and he leapt into a strange looking machine.

"My plantmobile is the fastest space vessel in the Universe, powered by supersonic plant gas. You'll never catch me," he laughed.

At the press of a button, an escape door in the laboratory opened and Tom looked up at the starlit sky.

"Goodbye, Major," shouted Plantro, and a platform began to raise the plantmobile to the sky.

Tom raced back up the ladder to Segment One.

"After him, Oddball," he commanded.

Plantro looked back as he sped off at fantastic speed. "You'll never catch me in that little machine," he cackled.

But as Plantro laughed he didn't notice one of the monster snapping flowers and his plantmobile crashed straight into it.

The flowery jaws closed tight as the Doctor screamed with anger, trapped by one of his own dreadful inventions.

Catching up in Segment One, Tom sent out the mechanical arm and grabbed Plantro's spaceship, pulling it clear of the ferocious, snapping plant.

"We can't have you gobbled up," chuckled Tom. "We still need the mixture to kill the weeds!"

Dr Plantro was forced to surrender and he gave Tom the instructions for making the mixture.

"Now we can free the Planet Rengo," said Oddball, proudly.

"Yes," added Tom. "And we'll put this villain behind bars. The only plants he'll see again will be the ones in the prison garden!"

SS Moon Cheese

Pisces

Little Bear

A Magnetic Field

Great Bear